Young Cam Jansen
and the
Double Beach Mystery

BY **D**AVID **A**. **A**DLER

ILLUSTRATED BY **S**USANNA **N**ATTI

SCHOLASTIC INC.

New York   Toronto   London   Auckland   Sydney
Mexico City   New Delhi   Hong Kong   Buenos Aires

For my friends at RO-JI,
thanks for the office.
—D. A.

To Grace and David Murray,
remembering summer days at Long Beach.
—S. N.

ISBN 0-439-48918-0

12 11 10 9 8 7 6 5 4 3 2 1   3 4 5 6 7 8/0

Printed in the U.S.A.   23

First Scholastic printing, May 2003

Set in Bookman

CONTENTS

Cam Jansen has an amazing memory. Do you?

Look at this picture. Blink your eyes and say, "Click!" Then turn to the last page of this book.

1. I HEAR THE OCEAN

"Listen," Aunt Molly said.

"Listen to this shell.

I hear the ocean."

Cam Jansen laughed.

"Of course you do," she said.

"We all hear the ocean.

It's right here."

"Oh," Aunt Molly said.

She took the shell from her ear.

"Well, I like this shell.

I'm keeping it."

"Here is another nice one,"

Cam's friend Eric Shelton said.

"I love seashells," Aunt Molly said.

"Let's find lots of them."

Aunt Molly told Cam's mother

that they were taking a walk.

"We're going by the water.

That's the best place
to find seashells."
Cam's mother was sitting
under a big red umbrella.
Cam and Eric took buckets
for their seashells.
Aunt Molly took a straw bag.

When they reached the water,

Aunt Molly turned.

She looked at all the umbrellas

on the beach.

"Oh my," she said.

"How will we remember

where your mother is sitting?"

Cam looked at

her mother's red umbrella.

She closed her eyes and said, "Click!"

Cam always closes her eyes

and says, "Click!"

when she wants to remember something.

"Mom's is the third umbrella

from the water.

An orange polka-dot umbrella

is in front.

When we come back,

we'll walk along the water.

We'll look for the

orange polka-dot umbrella.

Behind it is a green umbrella.

Then there's Mom's."

"Orange polka-dot umbrella,"

Aunt Molly said.

"Orange polka-dot umbrella,"

she said again.

"I have to remember that."

"Don't worry," Eric told her.

"Cam will remember.

She has an amazing memory.

Her memory is like a camera."

Cam says she has pictures in her head

of everything she's seen.

Click! is the sound her camera makes.

Cam's real name is Jennifer.

But because of her great memory,

people called her "The Camera."

Soon "The Camera" became just Cam.

2. SOMEONE IS LOST!

It was windy.

As Cam, Eric, and Aunt Molly

looked for shells,

beach balls, straw hats, and papers

blew past them.

They walked by the water.

Water washed over their feet.

"Hey! Stop!" they heard a boy shout.

The water didn't stop.

It washed over his sand castle

and ruined it.

The boy kicked the water.

He cried.

"Why did he build

so close to the water?" Eric asked.

Cam told Eric, "I bet

the sand here was dry

when he built his sand castle."

"The tide is rising,"

Aunt Molly said.

"The water keeps coming in."

Cam, Eric, and Aunt Molly

found lots of seashells.

"My bucket is full," Cam said.

"Let's go back."

"Mine is full, too," Eric said.

"But my bag isn't full,"

Aunt Molly said.

"Let's keep looking."

Cam and Eric helped Aunt Molly

find more seashells.

When her bag was full,

they started back.

Cam looked for the

orange polka-dot umbrella.

She didn't find it.

"We're not there yet,"

Cam told Eric and Aunt Molly.

"We have to keep walking."

They walked until they were almost

at the end of the beach.

They didn't find

the orange polka-dot umbrella.

"We're lost," Eric said.

"Oh no," Aunt Molly told him.

"We're not lost.

I know where we are.

We're on the beach."

"But where is Mrs. Jansen?"

Eric asked.

"I don't know where *she* is,"

Aunt Molly said.

"*She* must be lost."

3. THE ORANGE POLKA-DOT UMBRELLA

Cam closed her eyes.

She said, "Click!

I'm looking at a picture

of the orange polka-dot umbrella.

There is a blue umbrella

on one side.

There is a purple-and-yellow umbrella

on the other side.

Those umbrellas are right in front,

near the water."

Cam opened up her eyes.

Cam, Eric, and Aunt Molly looked again.

They didn't find

the orange polka-dot umbrella

or the others.

Cam closed her eyes again.

She said, "Click!

The woman sitting under

the orange polka-dot umbrella

is wearing a blue bathing suit."

Water washed over Cam's feet.

"Behind her," Cam said,

"is a green umbrella.

Behind the green umbrella

is Mom's red umbrella."

Water washed over Cam's feet again.

Cam opened her eyes.

She looked at the ocean.

She turned and looked at the people

sitting under umbrellas.

"That's it!" Cam said.

"We're *not* lost.

I know why we can't find

the orange polka-dot umbrella."

4. WHERE ARE MY PAPERS?

"Do you remember the boy

with the sand castle?" Cam asked.

"I remember," Eric said.

"The water ruined his castle."

Aunt Molly said,

"The boy built his castle

during low tide.

Now it's high tide."

Cam said, "The woman

with the orange polka-dot umbrella

sat close to the water

during low tide.

When the water moved in,

she had to move back.

Mom's umbrella should be

closer to the water now."

Cam, Eric, and Aunt Molly turned.

They walked and looked.

"There's a green umbrella," Eric said.

"There's your mom's red umbrella."

Cam, Eric, and Aunt Molly

ran to Mrs. Jansen's umbrella.

She was asleep.

"Here we are," Aunt Molly said.

"We found lots of great shells."

Mrs. Jansen opened her eyes.

She looked

at Cam, Eric, and Aunt Molly.

She smiled.

Then she looked beside her towel.

"My papers!" she said.

"What happened to my papers?

I put them right here,

and now they're gone."

"Wow!" Eric said.

"We already solved

one beach mystery.

Now we have another one!

This is some day!

It's a double beach mystery day."

5. LET'S SWIM

"I need those papers.

They're for my job," Mrs. Jansen said.

"I put them next to my towel.

I put a rock on top

so they wouldn't blow away."

"But they did," Eric said.

"This is a big beach.

We may never find them."

"But we'll look," Aunt Molly said.

"The wind is blowing that way,"

Eric said, and pointed.

"Let's go," Aunt Molly said.

Eric and Aunt Molly started to walk off.

"Stop!" Cam told them.

"Don't go anywhere.

I know where the papers are.

They're where Mom left them."

Aunt Molly laughed.

"This time you're wrong.

There are no papers here."

"Oh yes there are," Cam said.

"Mom put a rock on the papers
to keep them from blowing away.
But she couldn't keep the sand
from blowing on top of her papers."

Cam dug in the sand.

The papers were there,
right where her mother had left them.

Aunt Molly told Cam,

"You're great at solving mysteries.

And solving mysteries is fun.

Now let's swim.

That's fun, too."

"That's a great idea,"

Mrs. Jansen said.

They all walked to the water.

"Wait!" Cam told them.

She looked at her mother's

red umbrella.

She closed her eyes

and said, "Click!"

Cam opened her eyes and said,

"Now I'll remember   .

where to find Mom's umbrella."

"Good," Aunt Molly said.

"I don't want your mother

to get lost again."

Cam, Eric, and Aunt Molly laughed.

"Hey," Mrs. Jansen said.

"I wasn't lost!"

"Oh, yes you were," Aunt Molly said.

"When we were looking for seashells

we knew where we were.

We didn't know where you were.

You were lost!"

Now, Mrs. Jansen laughed, too.

Then they all ran to the water.

Aunt Molly kicked and splashed.

She had lots of fun.

Cam, Eric, and Mrs. Jansen

had lots of fun, too.

A Cam Jansen
Memory Game

Take another look at the picture on page 4.

Study it.

Blink your eyes and say, "Click!"

Then turn back to this page

and answer these questions:

1. What color is Cam's swimsuit?
2. Are there stripes or dots on Aunt Molly's swimsuit?
3. Is Cam wearing sunglasses? Is Eric?
4. How many people are wearing hats?
5. Who is holding a bucket, Cam or Eric?